Thanksgiving

Story and pictures by **Miriam Nerlove**

ALBERT WHITMAN & COMPANY, NILES, ILLINOIS

For Arnold, with special thanks to Judith and Karen.

OTHER BOOKS BY MIRIAM NERLOVE

Christmas

Easter

Halloween

Hanukkah

Passover

Text and illustrations © 1990 by Miriam Nerlove.
Published in 1990 by Albert Whitman & Company,
5747 West Howard Street, Niles, Illinois 60648.
Published simultaneously in Canada
by General Publishing, Limited, Toronto.
All rights reserved.
Printed in the United States of America.
10 9 8 7 6 5 4 3 2 1

Library of Congress Cataloging-in-Publication Data

Nerlove, Miriam.
Thanksgiving / story and pictures by Miriam Nerlove.
p.   cm.
Summary: A boy and his mother bake two pumpkin pies and go to
Grandma's house for a traditional Thanksgiving celebration.
Includes a brief overview of the first Thanksgiving.
ISBN 0-8075-7818-5
[1. Thanksgiving Day—Fiction. 2. Stories in rhyme.] I. Title.
PZ8.3.N365th 1990   89-49363
[E]—dc20   CIP
                                                              AC

Thanksgiving! It's time for Thanksgiving!

Each year in November we like to remember...

the Pilgrims, who came such a long time ago,
to build and to live here, to work and to grow.

They hadn't much food and the winter was cold.
The Pilgrims got sick—both the young and the old.

But Native Americans knew what to do.
The Pilgrims were taught many things that were new.

They grew corn and pumpkins to last the whole year.
They also caught fish, hunted turkey and deer.

The people were thankful for food they had grown...

so they held a great feast with plenty to eat.
There was cornbread and nuts, berries and meat.

Then neighbors and Pilgrims gathered to share
the Thanksgiving meal they all had prepared.

Now we remember that feast our own way,
with the special big dinner we're having today.

We work in the kitchen, Mommy and I,
and bake not just one, but *two* pumpkin pies!

We're off to Grandma's. "Mommy, let's go!
Please hurry up—we're going too slow."

The warm pumpkin pies smell so good and so sweet,
I sneak a small piece of the piecrust to eat.

We finally arrive at a little past four—
the whole family's waving at Grandma's front door.

There's Grandma and Minnie, her little gray cat,
Uncle Bob, Aunt Marie, cousins Laura and Matt.

We sit down to eat in a wonderful mood.
We say that we're thankful for plenty of food.

Uncle Bob carves the turkey and uses a knife
that is one of the biggest I've seen in my life!

We gobble the food down, we eat till we're stuffed.
When Grandma says, "More?" we tell her, "Enough!"

But, now comes the pie—and I know that it's good.
I waited to eat it as long as I could.

When we're finished with dinner, it's time to clean up—
Watch out! Baby Laura has Uncle Bob's cup!

I pick up the wishbone that's dried on a dish.
Matt and I pull—will Matt get the wish?

I win!
I make my own wish and I know what to say:
May next year's Thanksgiving be just like today!

(7 DAY LOAN - THANKSGIVING)

E

Nerlove, Miriam
Thanksgiving

	DATE DUE	
NOV 11 1998		

2/91